To Nathan, Nicole, and Gwen
—J.J.

For Maguire and Carter
—B.S.

Text copyright © 2016 by Jory John
Jacket art and interior illustrations copyright © 2016 by Bob Shea

Visit us on the Web! randomhousekids.com
Educators and librarians, for a variety of teaching tools, visit us at RHTeachersLibrarians.com

Library of Congress Cataloging-in-Publication Data is available upon request.

ISBN 978-0-385-38990-7 (trade) — ISBN 978-0-385-38991-4 (lib. bdg.) — ISBN 978-0-385-38992-1 (ebook)

MANUFACTURED IN CHINA
10 9 8 7 6 5 4 3 2 1
First Edition

Book design by John Sazaklis

QUIT CALLING ME A MONSTER!

JORY JOHN
wrote the words

BOB SHEA
drew the pictures

RANDOM HOUSE 🏠 NEW YORK

Quit calling me a monster!
Just . . . stop it, right this minute!

Just because I have a huge, toothy smile that glows in the dark.

Just because
I roar.

And
scream.

And
holler.

And whoop.

And cackle.

And howl at the moon.

And howl at the sun.

Just because I hide under the bed . . .

. . . or at the back of the closet . . .

. . . or behind the shower curtain . . .

. . . or in the glove compartment.

"Mommy, save me from that monster!"
you holler when I'm just trying
to get some groceries.

"I think there's a monster under my bed!"
you scream when I'm just trying to sleep.

Okay, so maybe I let my claw slip out.
And maybe I growl in my sleep.
But it's not my fault.

You should see *you* when you sleep.

BWHAHHHH BLARGH! BLOOP
BLOOOT! WUGGHT!
BLUP! BWAHHH!
SNORT! BLURP-SNORT!
BLORT! BWHATT!
SNORT! BWHAAT!
BLUP!

It's all so very annoying.
It's not like I ever call you names, do I?

I could easily be like,
"Look at that little meat
snack over there."

Or "There goes the kid I'm going to chomp up."

But I don't.
I don't say anything. Because I have good manners.
You could really learn something from me.

Yep. I'm a monster with excellent manners!

Um . . . I didn't mean . . .
I didn't mean *monster,* exactly . . .
I'm not a . . . um . . .

Sigh.

Okay, okay. Okay! I'm *technically* a monster.

**After all, I have horns. And fangs. And wild eyes.
And crazy hair. And clompy feet. And long toenails.
And a huge, toothy smile that glows in the dark.**

And my *parents* are monsters.
It's all kind of obvious, I guess.

Still, I really don't like being called
a monster one bit.

How would you like it?

You wouldn't—*that's* how.

So quit calling me a monster,
everyone.

My name is Floyd.
Floyd Peterson.

**That's the roar of Floyd Peterson.
Not bad, right?**

Now I'm going to bed.

Try not to wake me when you clomp in
with your silly feet. No offense.

ROAR
SNORE

ROAR
SNORE

Daddy, I think there's a monster in my closet!

No, son, it's just Floyd Peterson.

Oh . . . okay. Good night.

Much better.